Emma's Visions

The Inauguration of Barack Obama

This book is dedicated to my mother,

Sarah Ruth Casey.

Love, Kim

Important terms to know:

President- This person is the leader of the United States of America. They are in charge of the laws and considered the Commander-in-Chief.

Barack Obama- He was the first black (African American) president of the United States. He was elected in November 2008 and inaugurated to officially take office in January of 2009. He served two consecutive terms.

Washington, D.C.- This is the capital of the United States. It's sometimes referred to simply as "D.C." It is where the White House and other government buildings and monuments are. This is also where the inauguration is held.

Inauguration- This is a ceremony where the elected president takes his oath of office and officially starts his presidential duties. This tradition is noted in the Constitution. It specifies that the 4-year term of each elected president of the United States begins at noon on January 20 of the year following the election. Each president must take the oath of office before they officially become the President of the United States.

Martin Luther King Jr. - He was a civil rights activist who was born January 15, 1929 and was killed April 4, 1968. He was the most visible spokesperson and leader in the civil rights movement that fought for the fair and equal treatment of all people of all races.

Present Day

It was already a long day, although it was only noon. Sarah and Emma had driven a long distance with their parents and grandparents to get dropped off for their first day of college. The two girls had been friends for a long time, and it was their second time together in Washington, D.C.

Emma looked at Sarah with a smile and asked, "Do you remember the first time we were in D.C. together?"

Sarah turned to Emma and replied, "Of course I remember! How can I forget? It was when we saw President Barack Obama get inaugurated in 2009. I also remember you were having those visions!"

Both girls smiled at each other, remembering when they were younger and attending the inauguration of the first African American President of the United States.

Sarah looked at Emma. "Is that why you chose political science as your major?"

Emma said, "Yes, political science is all about government and politics. Being there all those years ago, in the capital of the United States to see the President, inspired me to want to learn more."

They were now 18 years old and going to college, but that day in 2009 had changed their lives!

Flash Back to January 19th, 2009

"Sarah, when are you going to start packing? You know how forgetful you are sometimes. Make sure you don't forget anything..." Emma whined, cutting her big brown eyes at her friend Sarah.

Sarah looked up at her friend as she took a break from feeding her doll to answer Emma.

"My mom always says the same thing. She made me pack my bag days ago, and I have everything!" She then began naming items while pointing to her fingers.

"I have my earphones, my tablet, clothes, my comfortable sneakers, my favorite cherry lollipops, my favorite pajamas, my pillow, and my Laura," pointing to the well-fed doll named Laura.

"Good!" replied Emma with a smirk on her face.

"Tomorrow is a big day, an important day! Grandma and Grandpa call it a his-tor-i-cal day." she said trying to pronounce the word correctly.

Sarah looked at Emma, confused.

"Grandpa always talks about Dr. Martin Luther King Jr. and how important he was to our country. Do you remember when we learned about him in school?" Emma questioned her friend.

Sarah nodded her head eagerly, wanting to hear more. She loved to hear Emma's stories.

"Well," Emma continued, "Grandpa said that Dr. King dreamed that one day African Americans would be equal and have equal rights. Since we will have our first black president now, this will be a part of history. So it's historical!" she smiled.

Both girls laid back on Emma's bed and thought about the trip to the inauguration and how special a day it would be. Before long, their thoughts lullabied them to sleep.

Although the girls were friends, they were more like sisters. Emma parents passed away when she was just 3 years old. When that happened she moved in with her grandparents. One of the happy parts about the move was that Sarah happened to live right next door to Emma's grandparents. The two became instant friends! They often slept over each other's house, went to the same school, and were both in the third grade. It was good to have somebody she could talk to about anything. *Anything*, sometimes included things that were a secret between just the two girls.

Another interesting thing happened after Emma's parents passed away. She started having visions that allowed her to see people who were no longer alive. She would close her eyes, and a whole story would take place in her mind. They weren't dreams. She was awake and these visions felt real to Emma. The people in the visions were always historical people who were not alive anymore, These people protected the people who were living, like guardian angels.

It was kind of like how Emma felt her parents watched over and protected her although they were gone. Sarah was the only person who knew about Emma's visions, and she promised to never tell anyone. That strengthened their bond and made them inseparable.

January 20th, 2009

The next morning the house was filled with a hustle and bustle while her grandparents packed the minivan for the trip to D.C., where the inauguration would be held. In an effort to stay out the way, the girls got dressed and went outside to play while Emma's grandparents and Sarah parents loaded the minivan for them to drive.

Sarah ran around the yard and suddenly realized Emma was no longer chasing her.

In fact, Emma sat very still against a tree in the yard with a blank stare. Most people would have tried to get her attention, but Sarah knew her friend so well that she could tell that Emma was having a vision!

Therefore, instead Sarah walked quietly to Emma and carefully held her hand and allowed her to have her vision peacefully. Minutes passed, and soon Emma shook her head and smiled as she came back to reality.

Sarah questioned her friend, "Tell me Emma, what did you see?"

"I saw Dr. Martin Luther King!" she said with a smile on her face. She continued, "He was pacing back and forth like he was waiting for something special to happen. He was dressed in a black suit with a crisp white shirt and black shoes. He was talking to someone but I couldn't see that persons face or hear their voice. Dr. King was talking a lot but I didn't make out everything he said. I just wish I knew who he was talking to so I would know who he was trying to protect and guide. The only thing I'm sure he said was, 'I'll be with you and your family and I'll never leave your side. You have a job to do.'"

"Wow," Sarah started, "I wonder who he was talking to? I can't wait until you have another vision so we can find out more!"

Soon after the vision ended, both families went inside and ate a quick breakfast together before getting into the minivan for the trip.

As they walked to the minivan, Sarah and Emma noticed that Emma's Grandmother was struggling to hold a gray tote bag on her lap. It seemed really heavy for her small arms but she refused help when her husband offered. She insisted on keeping the bag close to her at all times. They thought it was odd but shrugged it off and got in the minivan.

Sarah's parents sat in the front seat. Emma's grandparents sat in the next row. And Sarah and Emma sat together in the 3rd row of the minivan in the back.

The ride from New Jersey to Washington, D.C. was long but entertaining. They listened to music from all the different generations that were in the car. Everyone took turns playing their favorite songs and making others guess who sang the song and telling each other interesting facts.

After a few hours of everyone enjoying themselves and music, the parents and grandparents went into their own conversations. At the same time, the girls chatted and giggled about different things.

When the two families arrived at the inauguration, they were excited to see how many people of all colors and backgrounds were there. Although it was cold, there were people on the streets playing music, selling tee-shirts and food. The smells of food perfumed the air. The food trucks lined the streets selling everything from bean pies to gyros. Some trucks sold tee-shirts and mugs that said President Obama's slogan, "Yes We Can."

There were people from all over the world speaking different languages. Even people who spoke English; spoke in so many dialects and accents that it sounded like music. The sights and sounds filled Emma and Sarah's souls as they and everyone else around them moved towards the Capitol Campus and closer to where the inauguration ceremony was actually being held.

"This is the day! Our his-tor-i-cal day! January, 20th, 2009!" Sarah exclaimed.

Everyone had a smile on their face. Emma watched her grandfather walk wearily but proudly towards the crowd with their tickets. There was lots of security to protect the president. Some were dressed in officer uniforms while others were in plain clothes. There were many speakers for the ceremony that sat at the head of the crowd on the inaugural platform. The inaugural events had actually started on January 18, 2009 and would continue for a few days, until the 21st. This day, January 20th was actually one of the largest gatherings, because it was the swearing-in ceremony where the new president would take his oath of office.

At the start of the event, there was a live band and then a prayer by Rick Warren. Then Emma's grandparents and Sarah's parents watched in awe as Aretha Franklin came out in a beautiful gray cloak and hat to sing "My Country 'Tis of Thee". She gave it a beautiful jazz twist that made it sound like a new song and gave it new meaning as she said, "freedom."

Sarah's mother looked down at the girls and said, "Now that's a voice!" Both girls shook their heads in agreement.

Joe Biden received an honor as he was inducted as the vice-president. Then there was a 21-gun salute as the presidency was passed from George Bush to Barack Obama. After what seemed like forever, it was finally time for Mr. Obama to come to the podium to make his speech and officially be made President of the United States.

On the stage, Barack Obama was sworn into office with his wife Michelle Obama and two daughters, Malia and Sasha. Both girls had big smiles on their faces while they watched two other little girls with the same brown skin they had, get inducted as the First Family of the USA. Sarah's parents beamed as they watched the President and First Lady. Emma's grandparents stood clutching each other with happy tears running down their faces.

"Grandpa and Grandma, why are you crying?" Emma asked.

Grandpa answered, "These are tears of joy baby girl. We never thought we would live to see this day, but it's here, we're here and our hearts are so happy."

Sarah who now sat high on her father's shoulders was turning her head back and forth in amazement of the amount of people that were there.

As the new President Barack Obama began to speak, Sarah got down from her father's shoulders. She looked over to Emma, whose head was tilted and eyes were staring into space like she always did when she started to have one of her visions. Sarah held Emma's hand.

Emma was about to have the vision that would put all the missing pieces together.

She saw a vision of Dr. King coming from the skies down towards the platform where President Barack Obama stood. No one could see or hear him besides Emma. His face beamed with light as he levitated in the air angelically.

Dr. King started to speak. Emma was the only person who could actually hear him, but she could tell that President Obama could sense his words. Today Dr. King spoke more words and was clearer than he was in her other vision. Emma heard him say:

"My son, your role is much different than mine. Everything I did in my time was so you could be here today. You will take on my fight to keep peace, unity and equality for all of God's people. I know you have a heavy burden and it will be difficult to please everyone, but if you keep love and peace at the top of your list, and you'll be fine.

You may be met with adversity, mistakes you will make, criticism you will take, but you will carry on. I'll be with you, as you create your own legacy as our first black president... I'll never leave your side."

Then Dr. King then took a neatly folded handkerchief from his suit pocket and wiped the tears from his eyes; and just like that, he was gone. The vision was over.

Emma sighed and smiled and her eyes shifted back to normal. As soon as President Obama was done speaking, the girls sat down with each other in the crowd to talk about the vision. Sarah listened to Emma tell her story. It was at that moment that they realized that Dr. King was talking to President Obama the whole time. He was his guardian angel and passed the torch so that President Obama could continue on with his work to help the country! Martin Luther King stood for peace and equality for all people.

Barack Obama being president of a country that was once so divided, showed that there was progress. Although there was more work to be done, Martin Luther King Jr.'s dream and fight for peace would be continued with Barack Obama.

Once the festivities were over, Sarah and Emma felt the cold air kissing their bare faces as they walked back to the minivan that was parked miles away. Although it was a far walk, it was more of a celebration. Once both families were snug into the van, Emma's Grandma reached into the tote bag she was still holding close to her body. She then took out a bible. Between the well-worn pages there was a picture of a beautiful woman with dark brown skin and jet black hair.

Emma squinted her eyes and asked Grandma, "Who is that?" Grandma had tears in her eyes as she explained, "This lady is my Grandmother Alexandria Jane, who raised me. I wanted to make sure that she got to see this extraordinary day. Although she couldn't be here in person, a part of her was here to see the first African American president. A man who will do good for all people of all races and beliefs."

Night fell as the families made it back to the hotel. Both girls looked out the window reflecting on the day. Sarah saw Emma looking at the moon. "Are you having a vision?" she questioned. "No," Emma stated, "Knowing Dr. King is watching over President Obama is enough for the day." She smiled with knowing eyes as they opened the minivan doors and skipped into the hotel.

The End

About the Authors:

Kimberly Casey- Bailey is from Plainfield, NJ. She graduated from Plainfield High School, then went on to work in the Plainfield and Rahway public school systems for over 23 years. Kimberly also worked for the Boys & Girls Club of Union County. She is married to John Bailey and they have one son, Johnathan Bailey. She holds a Bachelor's Degree in Criminal Justice with a minor in Sociology and is passionate about racial equality and social justice. Kimberly is currently working on her auto-biography. She enjoys spending time with family, playing softball and trivia games.

Shanice Young is a Creative from New Jersey. She is a certified Learning Professional who works in training, instructional design and coaching. She holds a degree in Business Administration and a degree in Liberal Arts. She loves creative writing and is passionate about education. She also is an event planner and creative designer for spaces and content. She has two smart and amazing sons, Lennox and Langston that continue to inspire her. To find out more, you can visit ShaniceTheCreative.com

About the Illustrator:

Tammy Nekita Lembrick is a New Jersey based artist. She has been sharing her art with the world since she could hold a pencil. She describes herself as self-taught but God given. Although this is her first book illustration, Tammy has taught art and painted murals across the state. The Artist is a devoted Mom of 3 awesome children who share and inspire her creativity. She is the owner of the Nekita May Art Company, and can be contacted at Tammy@nekitamay.com

Special thanks to Professor Abigail Perkiss

for her encouragement.

Special thanks to (Tina) Marie Johnson from Shanice; for

always encouraging creativity and writing.